✓ **W9-AAX-476**

KATHERINE ZECCA

A Puffin's Year

DOWN EAST BOOKS

To Ann Marie Zecca

ISBN (10) 0-89272-742-X ISBN (13) 978-089272-742-1

Library of Congress Cataloging-in-Publication Data

Zecca, Katherine.
  A puffin's year / by Katherine Zecca.
      p. cm.
  ISBN-13: 978-0-89272-742-1 (trade hardcover : alk. paper)
  1. Atlantic puffin—Life cycles—Juvenile literature. I. Title.
  QL696.C42Z42 2007
  598.3'3—dc22

                            2006032809

Typography by Lurelle Cheverie
Printed in China

5   4   3   2

Down East Books
A division of Down East Enterprise, Inc.
Publisher of *Down East,* the Magazine of Maine
Book orders: 1-800-685-7962   www.downeastbooks.com

On a cool spring evening, a colorful beak of bright orange and yellow appears in the waters of the Atlantic Ocean. A face of mostly white feathers follows. This is an Atlantic puffin. He has many other names, too, such as "parrot of the sea" and "clown of the ocean."

For seven months, this puffin has been at sea, living through storms and lots of cold weather. He spends most of his life on the water, only coming to land each spring, to nest.

Together, he and his mate will raise one chick this year—their puffling.

Near the nesting ground, the puffin and his mate join a large flock of other puffins. It is an exciting time when all the puffins flap their wings, dive, and splash as they greet each other in this once-a-year ritual.

AWW-aaah, aaah-aaah-aah-ah!

Papa puffin has found his mate. Seeing each other for the first time, they call out with a nasal grunting sound. Mama puffin, her black feathers shining, flicks her head, stretches her neck up and answers: *AWW-aaa, aaah-aaah-aah-ah.*

They swim slowly around each other, softly touching bills. Turning their heads side to side, feathers ruffled, they nod to each other in courtship.

Then, all at once, as if someone had yelled "*Go*," the entire flock of puffins leaps from the water and flies to solid ground.

Today is a big day. With a roly-poly walk, the puffin pair stroll about the colony together as their romance continues on this island home of theirs.

Two male puffins both want the same spot for their nest burrow. They stomp their feet and open their bills wide. They puff their cheeks and bodies to look bigger. Other puffins gather to watch. Locking beaks, the two males try to wrestle each other down, using their feet and wings in a noisy battle.

Suddenly, the flock scatters as black-backed gulls swoop down.
Sploosh! One gull nearly catches a puffin!

Mama and Papa puffin flap their wings and head
to the water, where they dive for safety.

When the gull has
left and the puffins feel safe
again, they hop and climb rocks to their burrow,
the same one they use every year. Other burrow holes dot
the hills all over the island. These narrow openings between
the rocks are future homes for pufflings soon to be hatched.

ARRR-ARRR-ARRR! Standing tall, with their tails up, Papa and
Mama puffin sound an alarm when they see a young male puffin
standing in the entrance to their burrow. They stomp their feet and
shake their heads as a warning to the stranger. The young puffin sees
that he is not welcome and flies away in search of another burrow.

Their nest hole needs repair. Papa puffin scratches and digs at the dirt with his claws, using his webbed feet as a shovel. Dirt flies out between his legs. Using his narrow, sharp beak like an ax, he makes the burrow wider.

The burrow runs deep below the boulders. It is curved, with a special space in the middle that will be used as a toilet by their puffling. At the far end of the tunnel, Mama puffin places soft grass and feathers to form a nest on the floor before she settles in to lay her egg.

Hidden from the light of day,
Mama puffin tenderly turns her
new egg, holding it between her
wing and body to keep it warm.

Both puffins take turns keeping the egg warm, guarding the burrow, and feeding each other during the next five weeks while they wait for their egg to hatch.

Papa puffin has returned from the sea with fish. He approaches the entrance and makes a series of clicking sounds. Mama puffin answers with a grunting noise.

Forty-one days later, an adorable, downy gray ball, with a white belly and two button eyes, appears. Their little puffling has hatched.

Deep in his safe burrow, the puffling eats fish and sleeps and grows bigger—

and **BIGGER,**

and *BIGGER!*

Papa puffin brings a snack of fish to his youngster. Then he yawns, shakes his feathers, and settles down in front of the burrow to protect the puffling from predators.

Nearby, Mama puffin is diving for small fish. One by one, she lines them up in a row, using the sharp edges of her beak to catch them. She can hold many fish at once with her beak and tongue.

Whee-er-er, whee-er-er! the puffling cries because he is hungry. Mama puffin arrives and lays her mouthful of live fish close to the front of the burrow.

Chip-chip-chip, the puffling responds as he scuttles to his food, eager to eat.

It has been forty days since the puffling hatched. Mama and Papa puffin stay nearby. They will continue to bring more fish, but he will refuse to eat. Somehow the puffling knows that it soon will be time for him to leave his safe island burrow and fly out into the big world.

Restless and excited, the puffling pokes his head out, closes his eyes, and feels the warm sun for the first time. A large shadow from above, maybe a gull, catches him by surprise and scares him. He pulls back inside. His burrow home is still the best place to be during the day.

At night, after it is good and dark, the puffling pokes his head out again. He looks around and sees no gulls. Other pufflings like himself sit near the entrances of their nest holes. They flap and stretch their wings, getting ready to explore their new world. Each night, he goes out again and ventures a little farther from home.

Then, one night, he and all the other pufflings dive into the water together, and their new life begins.

All on his own, without his parents, the puffling will have to learn how to catch fish and how to stay safe. Instinct is his best companion.

Mama and Papa puffin and the other adults spend the rest of the summer on the island, resting, eating, and getting ready for another long winter at sea, far from any land.

Two or three years later, a need to return to the island will touch their puffling. Maybe, when he arrives, he will dig his burrow near his parents' as they repeat the cycle of the puffin's year.

PUFFINS AND PEOPLE

With their upright stance and colorful bills, puffins are certainly among the most appreciated of all birds. But they also should be admired as rugged seabirds that are equally at home bouncing over frothy seas or burrowing underground to create a nest for the single chick they raise each year. After studying puffins for more than three decades, I am still in awe of these dynamic creatures.

Because they spend most of their time at sea and nest on remote islands, puffins may seem far away from us. But their future depends on *our* everyday actions. It is up to us to keep the oceans safe from oil and chemical spills and to halt the global warming trend that threatens our beautiful planet.

As Earth stewards, it's our job to stay informed about conservation issues and to vote for environmentally responsible lawmakers. If we truly care about the puffins and their marine world, it is very important to support sustainable fisheries, use less energy, create less waste, and recycle more. Working together, we can take actions that will make a huge difference for puffins and for all life on Earth.

PROJECT PUFFIN is one example of how people can make a positive difference for wildlife by taking action at the local level. This National Audubon Society program is dedicated to restoring nesting populations of puffins and other seabirds in places where they have become rare or extinct. Project Puffin is responsible for managing rare seabird colonies at many Maine coast islands. The techniques we've developed have been used to help more than forty species of birds in twelve countries worldwide.

To learn more about seabird research, education programs, visiting Maine puffin colonies, and our "Adopt a Puffin" program, write us at Project Puffin, 12 Audubon Road, Bremen, ME 04551, or visit our Web site: www.projectpuffin.org. Thanks for caring!

Stephen Kress
DIRECTOR, PROJECT PUFFIN